Primary Source

A Star Circ Adventure

Steve Rzasa

www.steverzasa.com

Books

The Interstice Universe
Remains
Mirages
Shivers
Mercury on Staff
Mercury First Up
The Echo Watch
Airfoil: Origins
Airfoil: Drake City
Mercury on Guard
Mercury for Hire
Mercury at Risk
Mercury is Hot
Mercury out Cold
Mercury off Course
Mercury with Style
Become the Past
Tangents
Interstice Undone
A Bad Guy

Fantasy
The Bloodheart
The Lightningfall
Just Dumb Enough
Crosswind & Sandstorm

Space Opera
The Face of the Deep
Unsettled
The Word Reclaimed
The Word Unleashed
Broken Sight
The Word Endangered

Vincent Chen series
Severed Signals
Cryptic Commands
Failed Frequencies
Mixed Messages

Marcus Verge
Verge of Peril

Takamo Universe
Empire's Rift
Strife's Cost
Counterstrike's Ruin

Star Circ
Primary Source

Books

Science-Fiction
Man Behind the Wheel
Reciprocity Road
For Us Humans
Eon City Burnout
The Null Razor Heist

Military Science-Fiction

Deception Fleet series
with Daniel Gibbs
Victory's Wake
Cold Conflict
Hazards Near
Liberty's Price
Ecliptic Flight
Collision Vector

Galaxy Bridge series
with Daniel Gibbs
Forward Command
Forward Hunt
Forward Pact
Forward Crisis
Forward Raid
Forward Shield
Reality Breaks
Reality Clash
Reality Restored

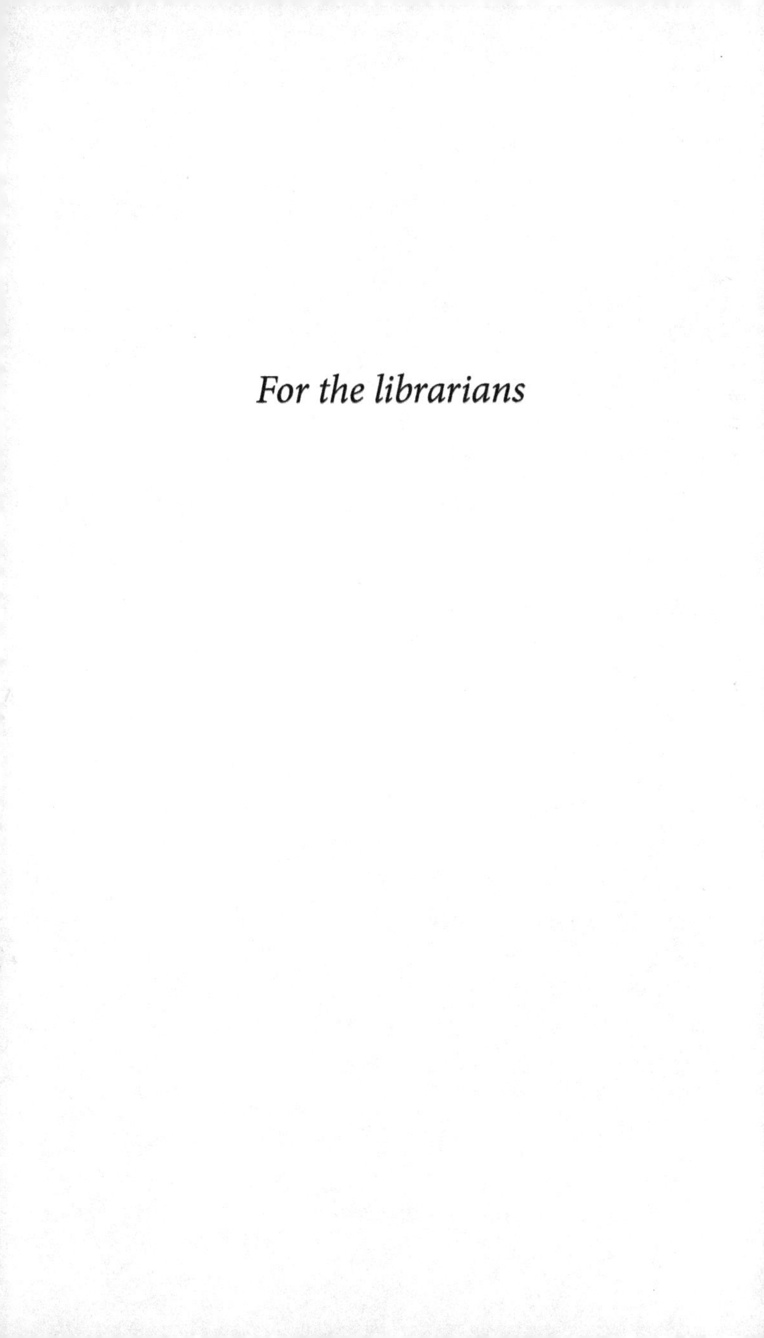

For the librarians

Sector 13112
Alguin Star System

Allied Archives Vessel Provenance
Three parsecs from the Alguin star

Bookship's narrative:
Galactic Standard Index 209.7.4.33

*This is Library Officer Second Class Callan Sark, recording on the First Librarian's behalf. ** Clears throat.** This is my first try at this, officially, so I hope I can be forgiven for any errors. ** Exhales. ** The bookship Provenance is on its way to the Alguin star system in hopes of recovering a vital codex, possibly more than one, belonging to the lost civilization of the Ka-Thos. Their society collapsed nine hundred years ago, leaving behind ruins and wreckage that have been picked clean by treasure hunters looking to make a fortune.*

Research obtained by Allied Archives Intelligence is convinced that the planet Alguin Five, as we call it, is home to one of the last Ka-Thos vaults untouched by pilferers. If the intel is right, we could be about to save a priceless set of records from destruction.

*** Long pause. ** The First Librarian has assigned me the retrieval mission. I've already been serving at the librarian's station on the bridge, so I've been on a few retrievals, but this one ... Well, let's just say that if I can't get these records, I'll be back to organizing new acquisitions while someone else takes the risks.*

Not this time.

Callan Sark found himself holding his breath, again. Not surprising. One false move could cause irreparable damage.

He gingerly lifted the wafer-thin slab from its place on the rack in front of him. The shelf label turned from green to red, showing the material in question had been removed, but a second later it blinked to yellow. The tracking system had confirmed that the removal was authorized.

That wasn't what had Callan on edge. His wariness stemmed from the fragility of the slab secured inside its stabilizing frame. It was ten times thinner than a typical sheet of paper in the collection, practically tissue, but far more fragile. Numbers downloaded and rose along the right side of the slab, where slightly thicker gray stone formed a second, sturdier frame. Flakes fell from the stone, littering the metal deck beneath Callan's shoes.

"Steady hands." Librarian First Class Winifred Akello stood a meter away, her hands clasped behind her back. Keen blue eyes were reflected in the glass wall surrounding the shelf unit, the eyes Callan always expected to be watching him, whether they were in the compartment with him or not. "But without fear. This part of your work is not life and death."

"It isn't," Callan said slowly as he turned toward the waiting cart. "I'd still like it to go well and without damage." He lowered it gently, imagining the slab was a sleeping baby. The thought made him smile. The last time he'd seen his brother, his nephew had stayed asleep while Warren patted Logan's back with vigor.

Wide slots lined the top of the white cart. Yellow lights pulsed beneath glossy black sides. Callan lowered the frame into the first slot and thought, *Come on. Engage the magnetic cocoon.*

The rim of the slot glowed blue. The frame wobbled out of Callan's hands and then disappeared down into the slot. <Item 171-311-112 secured for transport to Restoration>, the cart said in a scratchy artificial tone, and then it rolled away on squeaky rubber wheels.

Callan wiped his forehead with the back of his gloved hands. "Well, that went better than expected. I'd still feel better if we had drones do this work. They handle cleanup, after all."

"It would be easier, but it would not be our way." Akello gestured at the drone that swept in at knee height, hovering on hidden antigravity nodules. The rounded white triangle with brown accents dropped down until it was centimeters over the flakes littering the deck and Callan's boots. The soft whisper of vacuums, followed by the faint buzz of a scan, took only a couple of seconds. "The handling of library materials should be done by sentient biological beings."

"I believe that too." Callan yanked off his gloves, smiling as he did. "I just meant that the drones feel much less stress about handling priceless writings before they're converted into easy-to-read volumes for everyone else."

"Well, I promise not to ask them as long as you don't, either." Akello laughed lightly.

Callan grinned.

"Bridge to Librarian Sark."

The voice of Captain Leslie Belmont was strong and smooth. It echoed from the silver rectangular emblem of the Allied Archives on Callan's jumpsuit chest. He touched it, and after it beeped in response, he answered, "Sark here."

"Mr. Sark, we're about to enter the Alguin system. It's your show to run, Librarian."

The jolt of adrenaline was enough to get

Callan sweating again. "Yes, ma'am, on my way."

Akello took him by the shoulders. "Stand for the words."

Callan nodded. He appreciated the confidence. It would be nice to plug it straight into his brain and have it take control of emotional and logical oversight. But he knew he'd have to get there on his own.

He headed out of the stacks to the starboard lift, said "Bridge," and settled against one curved side of the cubical space as it shot upward. The lift compartment had transparent sides, which gave Callan an always intriguing view of the bookship's inner workings between its decks.

Light flooded the lift. Callan gazed out at rows of books, parchments, scrolls, tome bricks, memory lattices, and myriad other forms of literature arranged in neat rows. He ascended through the next seven decks, watching as drone cars shuttled volumes back and forth. Enlisted shelftechs conversed between stacks as they sorted volumes and shelved books fresh from retrieval to restoration, and inspected new acquisitions, their fragile forms held aloft in pale blue antigravity force fields

The *Provenance* was currently carrying twenty thousand items in its library module, about four-fifths its total capacity. It wouldn't make the trip to the main archives at Drai Ghell-Adams Starport until Callan returned with the Ka-Thos codices, at which point most—but not all—of the originals would be offloaded. Then the bookship would continue on its mission throughout the spin sectors of this slice of the galaxy: Collecting rare works to be translated and copied for dissemination and sharing among the Free Worlds for Information and its partner nation, the Pan-Stellar Consociation.

Callan's uniform jacket had bunched around the middle. He straightened it, smoothing out wrinkles. He ran a finger around the inside of his collar.

The responsibility of his position was enough to make him wish he could hide the rest of the voyage in the library module. But he told himself that anxiety would disappear as soon as he could get down to the planet's surface.

No place he'd rather be than on a retrieval.

The lift wall went dark as it slowed through the next few decks on its approach to the bridge. A chime sounded, and then the doors opened onto the *Provenance's* nexus.

Captain Leslie Belmont paced the half-circle of consoles arcing across the front of the bridge. She gazed at the big rectangular monitor that displayed the tiny bright light of the Alguin sun.

"Disengage the strings," Belmont ordered.

"Aye, Captain, disengaging." Helm sat far ahead of Scan One and the automated navigational array, halfway to the viewscreen from the captain's chair. The glowing sphere of grid lines and obstacle markers enveloped the helm officer in pale blue light. She eased her hands forward, her touch gentle against the twin control stems protruding from the base of her upright couch.

The *Provenance* trembled around them for a few seconds as the gravity drives powered by the dual cosmic strings at the heart of the bookship's power and propulsion accelerated them toward the planet. Callan settled against his chair's cushions, watching as the *Provenance* grew closer to the planet.

Belmont's right hand patted a soft rhythm against her left's palm as she continued her pacing. The movement reminded Callan of a watchful hunter stalking prey. "Scanners, what do we have?"

"Class Three lifeform readings and below, ma'am," the young woman seated at Scan One said. "No indication of sentient activity. Fauna reads as primarily reptilian DNA base. Flora measures at Point Eight Seven on the Terran biome scale."

"Very good. Librarian, piece it together."

That's me. Callan swept the Scan One readings from the data stream spilling down the right side of his flat paneled console into his duty station library, collating mission data as he went—cooldown rate for the dual string drive that propelled the bookship across the light-years; scatter falloff from the navigational screens and defensive energy shields; frequencies used by the communications arrays as they probed for local transmissions. He checked every item for patterns that might be useful to the retrieval and partitioned the data by subject and relevance, building the ship's narrative for eventual cataloging.

"While we're waiting," Belmont said, "Helm, take us into standard orbit for this category of planet. Acceleration to forty."

"Aye, Captain."

Callan watched his display as the schematics of the *Provenance* glowed. The ship was, at 400 meters long, typical of its class, and at 48 years old about halfway through its lifespan extended through hull regeneration and operational upgrades. It was a sleek ovoid, reminding Callan of a shining silver jewel with white paneling and blue accents lining key sections of its outer skin. The dual string drive stabilizers were separated from the hull by a series of interlocking connectors, allowing the cosmic strings to be exposed to and linked with space-time. A faint red shimmer occasionally emitted crimson flashes like summer lightning above the clouds.

"Skipper, I'm picking up severe atmosphere instability," Scan One commented. Her announcement jolted Callan from his reverie. "Electromagnetic distortions are off the charts. The activity is centered a hundred kilometers west of the target site, coming off the nearest oceanic body. Estimated landfall at the target site is one hour and forty-seven minutes."

Belmont glanced at Callan, pale gray eyes even more brilliant against dark brown skin. "Still waiting, Librarian. There can't be any question of the coordinates."

Callan grimaced. He'd been distracted by the elegance of the crew's ship handling and tried to ignore the heat creeping up past his collar. "Understood, Captain." He spoke in a calm, level voice he knew the ship's commanding officer needed in a moment like this. *Your job is to give her all the information she needs to make the decision. Advise, not dictate.* Akello's training filtered up through his colliding thoughts. "Library Intelligence assures me their informants on this case have their highest confidence. They rate the probability of the codices' location being at those coordinates at ninety-three percent, give or take two percent margin of error. "

"Hmm." Belmont pursed her lips. "That's a margin I can live with, but I'm not the one guiding a shuttlewing and its crew into a potentially fatal atmospheric storm. It's those extra percentages that bothers me."

"Captain, I understand those concerns, but there's an even better chance Stratnor gets its hands on those codices, and we lose them forever if we don't retrieve them." Callan's heart fluttered. His anxiety pulsed through him faster than a neutron star's core spun. The Strategic National Oversight Republic held the fanatical view that nothing unapproved by the state—namely, them—could infect the minds of pure humans. They chose any and all means to keep that dissemination from happening.

Callan shivered at the thought of Stratnor catching them. *We could all be destroyed along with the collection.* But it was a risk they had vowed to take.

Stand for the words.

"No need to trot out that bogeyman, Mr. Sark. The day I let Stratnor atomize another irreplaceable tome is the day I toss my stripes." Belmont turned toward the monitor. Her rank insignia shined under the dim bright lighting. "All right, take your team. You have your time limit. Get down there, check out the codices, and bring them back for A and C. We'll talk circ later."

"Yes, ma'am." Green lights blinked on at the corners of the hexagonal bridge: Acceleration phase ended. Callan rose from his seat and yanked one of three clear plastine catalog card blades from the left edge of his console. The card blade was a flat rectangle with the upper right corner sheared off at an angle, completely transparent except for the green glow around the edges and a faint spiderweb of gold circuit traceries. He squeezed the upper corner, where the print sensors hid. Reams of data gathered by Scan One and the rest of the *Provenance's* systems filled the lower half and a map of Alguin Five filled the upper.

"Mr. Sark?"

"Yes, ma'am?"

"Try not to blow anything up," Belmont said dryly. "And bring back my crew."

Callan smiled. "Yes, ma'am. I don't have any intention of damaging equipment."

"Oh, nobody ever has the intention, Librarian." Belmont shook her head and sighed. "It just kind of happens."

Callan nodded again and headed for the lift. This wasn't just a chance to preserve a lost civilization's last remaining records from galaxy-wide information suppression.

If Stratnor might be coming for those records, and a storm was bearing down, his mission became a race.

The lift doors opened onto the *Provenance*'s hangar bay, where the ship's complement of a dozen shuttlewings was nestled in three staggered rows facing the aft doors. Commander Gustav Aguilar, the ship's first officer and Captain Belmont's right-hand man, was waiting for him with a mobile equipment cart standing by.

"Sir." Callan stopped and braced himself to attention. The observance of protocol gave him plenty of time to catch his breath.

"At ease, Librarian." Aguilar opened the front panel of the MEC, revealing stacks of scanners, medkits, and survival gear. And, of course, weapons. "Your pilot and shelftech are already aboard. "Pulsons have had their discharge frequencies modulated to avoid getting scrambled by the planet's electrical interference. You'll need a rebreather for this one, too."

"Thank you, sir." Callan took a clear rebreather mask from the row hanging in the MEC, along with a dark blue field jacket lined with white, and made sure his equipment was stowed in the proper pouches of his excursion backpack.

"Here." Aguilar gave him a pulson in its holster. "There's no local fauna to worry about, according to Scan One, but if Stratnor shows up …" He left the meaning hanging in the air.

Callan looked at him. Stocky, with curly

gray hair and a thick mustache, Gus Aguilar bore a scarred patch of slick skin on the right side of his face. The story went that he'd held off a Stratnor burn squad by himself for two days before he could be retrieved, and when he was, the rescue squad found him sagging against a ruined outpost wall, clutching a bundle of stained parchment in one hand and a hand pulson in the other, The six Stratnor attackers were strewn in various stun states all around him.

Callan accepted the nonlethal weapon, checked its charge, and fitted the holster to his belt. "Sir? Can I ask you a question?" It was Aguilar's role to personally prep retrieval teams, after all, so if anyone aboard knew how to handle what Callan might be facing, it was him.

"Anything, Sark."

"Stratnor … They won't get past the ship. Right?"

Aguilar frowned. "I'm not going to soften the blow, kid. Our sensors are good. But their stealth capabilities are tough to match. And you know the protocol: if the library collection is in danger—"

"The bookship's duty is to safeguard it first."

"And the retrieval team second."

Callan nodded glumly. *What were you expecting? This is part of the training, too. Maybe you were hoping for a way out.*

"Look, Librarian, the captain's not going to give up on you." Aguilar slapped him on the shoulder so hard he thought he might fall over. "So do your job."

"Yes, sir. Thanks, Commander."

Callan trotted down the row to Wing Five, slipped in through the angled hatch unfolding from the dagger-shaped spacecraft, and settled into one of the jump seats. He made sure to do it quickly, before his doubts had another chance to push him back out of the airlock.

His team was already inside and strapped in as the shuttlewing's engines rumbled to life. Warrant Officer Rito Yashida nodded from the cockpit as he flipped switches and tapped panels. He was a compact, muscular man a few years older than Callan with thick black hair swept back like a sleek helmet. Gray shock webbing held him in place. Curved display screens made up for the lack of physical viewports, though once the shuttlewing entered the planet's atmosphere, the featureless cockpit bulkheads would open up, allowing a clearer view of the sky.

"Morning, sir." Shelftech Second Class Lilou El Tayib, tall and slender like a long-distance runner, leaned her heavy pulson between her legs, the wide polished surface of its muzzle aimed at the deck. Dark brown eyes squinted at the pair of fresh charges she inserted into the stock, sending the small cylinders deeper into the white and black rectangular weapon. Blue indicators flickered to life along both sides. "Another day, another book hunt."

"Hopefully a successful one." Callan flinched as the shuttlewing shot forth from the *Provenance*, accelerated by magnetic pulse emitters mounted in the hangar ceiling. Cockpit screens showed the planet's rusty curve ahead and the curved hull of the *Provenance* behind, the starry background visible between the ring drive gaps in the center of the ship.

"Did you get the pep talk from Gus?" El Tayib asked.

"I did, though I think he could work on his reassurance." Callan inspected his hand pulson. He'd used it before on errant wildlife, and knew it would have no lasting effects other than lingering pain. Of course, he'd never shot a person, either.

"Don't worry, sir." El Tayib tightened her straps, then fitted her cap snug over bright blue hair "We've got to land first without crashing."

Yashida blew air between his teeth as he reached overhead and adjusted a control. "I think I'm offended."

A few minutes later the shuttlewing bounced through the whipping winds that scarred the coastal plains of Alguin Five's largest continent. Callan peered out of a triangular viewport at the black clouds on the horizons. Scratches and streaks smeared red electrical discharges into brighter blobs.

"This is what we call in piloting circles

Nas. Tee." Yashida clung to the control stick. Muscles on his forearms tightened as he banked the atmospheric craft into a starboard dive that had Callan clinging to his seat cushion, safety straps or not.

"Careful, Rito," El Tayib warned, the teasing evident in her tone and her grin. "You make the librarian puke and you'll be dusting old scrolls in the secure archive hold."

Yashida snorted. "That's not true … is it, sir?"

Callan chuckled as he plotted the map of the local landing site onto his catalog blade. A red rectangle appeared in the midst of hills, ledges, and ruins, courtesy of scan overlays he collected from the *Provenance*. "I don't have a problem with motion sickness, Mr. Yashida. Just get us on the ground so we can retrieve the codices before they're lost."

"Why's Stratnor even bothering with these?" El Tayib strapped a rebreather over her face, covering her eyes, nose, and mouth. Her voice came out tinny through the embedded speakers. Callan fitted his own rebreather and tested the seals. The air he sucked in smelled fresher already. "They don't need a reason, Shelftech. I have no doubt they'd vaporize the site from orbit with at-mat weaponry if they thought it would get the job done. It's entirely possible the codices are hidden deep enough that the electromagnetic storm coming our way won't harm them but given what little we know about the Ka-Thos civilizations on this continent, there's always the chance they could be irreparably damaged."

"Terrifying storms. Anti-matter bombs. Missing books." Yashida chuckled and shook his head. "It's never boring, eh, sir?"

Never boring? As far as Callan was concerned, it was more nerve-wracking than anything else, but he was glad to be able to put on a calming air. "No, Warrant, it never is."

"Well, just so long as we're clear." El Tayib leaned her head against the upper cushion of her seat and closed her eyes. "Me, I'll just be happy to stun a Stratnorguard into drooling numbness and swipe the books or codices or whatever right out from under their noses."

Callan heartily agreed but at that moment he was focused on what clues Library Intelligence had been able to collect about the target codices. They were potentially five thousand years old and made of a resin base that was durable beyond belief when encased in a neutral medium but highly susceptible to rapid degradation when exposed to electromagnetic disruption.

But Stratnor doesn't know that, or else they might just risk wasting an at-mat bomb on a target like this. As it is they have to make sure they eliminate the volumes firsthand. That means burn squads.

He shifted in his seat and, as he did, felt a weight press against his right ribs. Callan frowned. He dug through the inner pocket and came up with a book.

"That's not overdue, is it?" El Tayib teased.

Callan chuckled. "No, it's got a few weeks left on it. *Treasure Island.* Have you ever read it, Shelftech?"

"No, sir, I lean toward botanical journals. There's no other way I'd be able to keep the cacti alive in my quarters."

"Your loss." Callan peeked at the last page he'd stuck a bookmark in, smiled again, then eased the book into the jacket. Maybe after this run he'd finally get a chance to finish reading it. Physical copies were prized among the Allied Archives, because with Stratnor on the hunt for every unapproved piece of media it could find, reliance on digital forms was overrated.

"Here we go," Yashida said. "LZ coming up, fifty seconds to touchdown, sir."

"Steady as she goes."

The shuttlewing bucked like it had hit a tremendous speed bump in the air. Callan touched a handhold over his head. He frowned toward the cockpit.

"Just a touch of turbulence," Yashida said. "Don't you folks worry. I'll put us onto the dirt like a butterfly in search of nectar."

Callan doubted Yashida had seen a butterfly outside of holographic recordings, if he'd ever seen one at all, but had no choice. His life was in the pilot's hands.

Yashida swept the shuttlewing across a broad plateau and into a tight turn that brought the craft to a near standstill. "Eyes on the LZ. Confirm coordinates."

A notification flashed yellow on the edge of Callan's card blade. He touched it. Numbers skittered across the transparent surface and settled into a ring in the lower left corner of the glowing terrain schematics. Callan centered the image on that ring. He flicked his own set of orange numbers from one of the dozens of menus at the bottom of the screen. They touched the yellow ring, merged, and turned green. "Coordinates confirmed."

"Okay, the terrain's a bit rough there. I'm putting us a klick east. Hold tight."

The shuttlewing dropped like a stone. El Tayib retched. She pressed her lips into a thin line and put the back of her right hand to her mouth. Her cheeks bulged.

Callan hid a smile. Who was going to puke? Not him. He reserved his worry for the state of the codices.

Engines whined through the fuselage. The craft shuddered, and then a tremendous *bang* rattled every single strap, latch, and bin, as well as the bones in Callan's body. A second later, everything went still, except for the dying moan of the engines and the hiss of grit blown against the shuttlewing's exterior by the approaching storm winds.

"That's it! Skids down. Dirt's up." Yashida lifted his goggles. He kissed the first two fingers of his left hand, reached up, and rubbed them against a stamped metal tag bearing the shuttlewing's serial number and the name of its assigned bookship. "Let's go find our books."

Thirty seconds later, the trio stepped into the airlock. They pressed their shoulders together to fit into the compartment, no bigger than a closet, clad in the blue and gray excursion jackets that mimicked their uniforms. Callan punched up the clearance code. A light turned red.

The outer hatch slid open. Wind blasted into the compartment, sending white grit swirling about them. It pelted their exposed skin but thanks to the masks, they could breathe unimpeded and mostly see. Callan lifted the card blade to his face, holding it vertical. The ring turned accordingly, marking a position seven hundred and fifty meters ahead and to their left. "Coordinates locked. This way."

His earpieces muffled the howl of the wind as their boots crunched across the dried, encrusted dirt. Callan led the way. El Tayib walked two meters off his right shoulder and a couple of steps behind, sweeping the gleaming muzzle of the heavy pulson this way and that. Callan knew she didn't intend a rhythm but to him she became a human metronome, or at least, what he imagined a metronome moved like based on the *History of Musical Mechanics* volume he'd rescued from Beta Virginis Delta.

Yashida followed farther behind and to Callan's left. He aimed his hand pulson in the same way, though with not as smooth a pattern as El Tayib. Callan kept his defensive weapon secured to his belt holster.

"Negative sentient contacts," El Tayib said. "Scanner's showing only local biologicals. Small ones. But I can't get orbital updates from the *Provenance*."

"Same here, sir," Yashida said.

The earpieces acted as comms devices, too, channeling their speech to each other, another advantage over the roar. Callan checked the timer on his card blade. Fifty-six minutes until the storm hit. *The approaching front is bad enough. We definitely don't want to be here when the worst arrives.* "Keep to our course. This way."

They followed a path among toppled heptagonal pillars, each one bigger in diameter than the next, until they gazed up at fallen chunks that were ten meters across. Most of the carvings had been scoured by the grit but Callan recorded what little he could. It was possible they could return for a complete archaeological workup. His mission orders were clear, though: the materials must be preserved.

The green ring on his device grew larger and larger. Callan stared at the shallow mounds rising up the hillside toward crumbling ledges. He slowed his pace and glanced about for an obvious entrance.

"Is this the place?" Yashida asked.

"It is," Callan said. "The Codex Septon of the Ka-Thos, specifically, the third Septon of their second planet-wide kingdom. The same cataclysm that destroyed their civilization may have ruined this structure."

He could only just make out the overlapping terraces, seven layers reaching along the edges of the collapsed cliffs. Seismic upheavals appeared to have shattered each layer and tipped them by at least ten degrees in many directions, none the original. Yet the coordinates were insistent—somewhere fifty meters ahead of them was the location of the codices.

El Tayib spun around. She hunkered into a crouch. "Contact." Her pulson angled up to the sky. "Aerial. Coming in fast."

The screech Callan had thought was the wind whistling through the ruins took on a more artificial edge. It grated at his ears, even through the protective comms earpieces, until a red glow appeared on the southeast horizon. *Good thing she was paying closer attention.*

"That's a Stratnor lander," Yashida snapped. "Mark Two Pollux. You can tell by the high octaves in the sound made by the maneuvering thrusters."

"We need cover," El Tayib said. "Librarian?"

"Under here." Callan jogged toward the nearest overhang where the second layer of pasty yellow stone was cantilevered up from the ocher layer beneath it. The dark gap was wide enough to admit a human crouched, so he shone the beamlight attached to his wrist into the shadows. Insectoids with fourteen legs scuttled out of reach, their gold shells shimmering like buried treasure. The slight weight of his book leaned against him. *Robert Louis Stevenson. An old, old story. Pirates and murder and greed.*

This wasn't the quite the same situation, but he found himself wondering if pirates would be preferable to Stratnor. At least pirates, in theory, could be bargained with.

He tried not to think of that as the angled fuselage of the Stratnor lander veered into view over the valley, wobbling from side to side.

"They're either coming in too fast and too low, or their pilot's been zapping himself with too many brain mods," Yashida muttered as he clambered into the gap alongside Callan.

El Tayib was last in, managing her entry backwards, the pulson still aimed skyward. She scowled. "If they see our shuttlewing we're stuck down here. Better get those books before we're permanent residents, Librarian."

"That is my plan, Shelftech. Keep our new patrons occupied while I search the stacks."

El Tayib snorted. Callan couldn't help smiling a bit at dropping the old jargon. It didn't apply to much out here on the desolate worlds, among the graveyards of distant civilizations laid bare by time and disaster. Still, it meant everything to their cause. He couldn't imagine not sharing the written word with as many sentient species as possible. Wanting to destroy it was beyond his comprehension.

The engine noise made a sudden crescendo. Yashida blurted a wordless sound of surprise. Callan twisted as best he could in the confines of the slanting gap, pressing his boot into a crevice between heptagonal bricks so that he could take a better look back outside.

The lander overflew the site again but sideways, reeling onto one side. It came far too close to the ground, as Yashida predicted, and clipped one of its four shallow V-shaped wings against a pillar that hadn't toppled. That was enough to throw it into a spin, the engines screaming for aid. The lander careened toward a cliff and ripped off another wing, trailing smoke and sparks, until it slammed into the ground on the other side of the Codex Septon ruins from where Callan, El Tayib, and Yashida were hidden. Thunder rumbled in its wake, replacing the engine noise, shaking dust free from the roof slanted over Callan's head.

"They could have survived," El Tayib said. "We should move quickly."

Callan nodded, though he felt sick to his stomach. People might have just died. Enemies or not, they were people, with families or loved ones. As much as Callan wished Stratnor would cease to exist, he didn't wish for their death.

He hoped for redemption instead.

"About that, Mr. Yashida …" Callan shifted his card blade. The green circle pulsed with an almost palpable eagerness. The coordinates were twenty meters below, down the slant of the layer on which they sat.

"Um," Yashida said. "That's not great."

"Buckle up, flyboy." El Tayib looped the carry strap of her pulson across her shoulder. She withdrew a set of climbing pitons from her belt, drove one deep into the seam between the bricks beneath her, and twisted the silver spike. It whirred, digging in deeper, then extruded four additional spikes that anchored it in place. She repeated the process with two more before clipping coiled lines to each. They glowed, their pale green strands dropping deeper into the dark. "I'll go first, sir."

Callan gestured with the card blade. El Tayib rappelled down the sloped floor like she'd being rock climbing her entire life. Of course, Callan knew shelftechs were trained at these high-priority retrievals the moment they enlisted, so he wasn't surprised by the skill with which she slid into the darkness. Impressed, yes. Worried? Still.

He went next. Momentary claustrophobia gave way to awe as he descended into the green gloom, surrounded by carvings much sharper and decipherable than those on the pillars outside. His boots crunched on stone debris a few seconds later. White light exploded, forcing him to blink as his eyes adjusted to the new brilliance.

El Tayib was using the lamp mounted under her pulson's barrel as a searchlight to clear the room they were in. The space was square, unlike the rest of the shapes outside and around them. And it was lopsided, as was to be expected given the cant to the floor. "Clear."

Clear, it was, except for the broken crystal rising from the center of the room. It too was heptagonal, though two sides and the top had been sheared off. Glittering fragments surrounded the object, which rose to chest height.

The codices sat undisturbed inside the

crystalline casing.

They were a pair of volumes only a few centimeters in diameter and one meter long. Their covers were made of a pebbly material that ranged in hue from bright orange to dull brown, with dozens of shades between and stripes at sharp angles. *Reptilian skin, by the looks of it.* Callan could see tattered bits of parchment or whatever passed for writing material—probably the resin his files made mention of—protruding from either end of each codex, with flakes stuck to the crystal. Some of those flakes bore faded scribbles.

Behind him, he heard scrabbling on paving as Yashida tumbled onto the floor. He winced and rubbed his lower back. "Lost my footing."

"Don't worry. We'll get you back in the cockpit soon enough." Callan was shocked he could manage the words, because he stared at the contents of the crystal until he was sure his eyes would stay stuck wide open.

Yashida whistled.

Callan thought that summed up the find nicely.

El Tayib looked up at him. "How are we going to get this out of here, sir?"

"Very carefully." Callan pulled on a pair of slim green gloves, the palms and fingers interlaced with silver crosshatching. He squeezed his hands together. The gloves emitted a faint, low hum, and grew much warmer, so much so his palms began to sweat. The backs glowed with the white number "1."

"This setting should be enough," Callan muttered, more to himself than the others. He brushed his hands along either side of the crystal formation. Wafers fell away, leaving a much smoother, but cloudier, layer of crystal, with bright edges. Steam rose into the thin air. "It can slice enough away to get them down to a manageable load."

So, he did, over the next few minutes. Eventually, all that remained of the crystal's upper section, which contained the codices, was a thin shell surrounding them. Callan shaped his slicing so that the portion supporting the codices grew narrower until he could deactivate the gloves and give what was left a gentle push.

The bottom cracked clean off. The codices, still encased in crystal, fell into Callan's waiting hand. They wobbled, the lump threatening to fall over, until Callan squeezed tighter and held them firm. Only once they were steady did he exhale.

"Nice work, sir." Yashida chose then to stop pacing. Callan had done his best to ignore the pilot's boots shuffling along the stone floor but now they were almost as loud as the tumult outside. "Permission to return us to the shuttlewing before it gets buried."

Callan chuckled. His giddiness tickled at his sense of humor and made his body feel half its weight, even with the crystal containing the codices strapped into a backpack slung between his shoulders. *Bounding up the rope won't be a problem at all.* He couldn't wait to get the codices back aboard the *Provenance* and into Collections where he and the shelftechs could strip the plastic away, opening up the documents for preservation. Only then could they run the translation algorithms and make 3-D physical copies for circulation.

"Up we go, people." In his euphoria Callan ignored the details of what El Tayib was saying about securing the entrance and so he wasn't alarmed at the sight of people waiting for him when he quickly climbed to the top, until he realized the men standing there weren't *Provenance* crew. For one thing, their uniforms were tan and green. For the other, half of them were AGU sentrybots.

"This had better be worth it." The leader, like the other two people flanking him, wore a reflective gold visor over his face. He was shaved bald, too, which Callan thought idly must help keep his hair free of grit. The man's voice rippled from speakers in a raspy, electronic wave. "Hand over the codices."

Callan didn't have a chance to comply because the three sentrybots—tall, gangly automatons lacking faces to their oblong heads and sporting four spindly arms—grabbed him. Hands with three pincers each plucked at his backpack and his belt, stripping away his cargo and his tools. His card blade flopped onto the dirt.

"Get off of me," Callan snapped, switching

to his external speaker so they could understand. "The Free Worlds for Information have a treaty with the Consociation stipulating—"

The leader plucked Callan's mask from his face. Callan caught the name "Li-Olsen" etched onto a black plate fastened to his chest. There were silver lieutenant's stripes on his shoulders.

He only had a second to catalog those details before grit swirled into his mouth and up his nose, causing him to cough and retch. Callan felt like he was gargling needles.

"The Pan-Stellar Consociation's reach has limits," Li-Olsen said. "Out here nobody cares. Out here the Strategic National Oversight Republic will do what it must in order to prevent dangerous, outmoded information from spreading throughout humanity."

"You're …" Callan coughed. He couldn't catch his breath. His vision clouded. Darkness pushed in around the sides of what he could see. Where were El Tayib and Yashida? "The freedom … of the people to share knowledge—"

"Don't lecture me, Librarian," Li-Olsen

snapped. "Degenerate writings like those created by the Ka-Thos are the same as what's been corrupting humanity for centuries, on and off Earth. Once we stamp this threat out, we'll take you back for reorientation into the true human race."

Light flashed on both sides of Callan. He thought it was from the effects of the storm-driven grit, and the atmospheric poisons, but then the two sentrybots holding him flopped onto the dirt, powerless.

El Tayib and Yashida. They'd finally chosen their moment to strike.

Callan fell backwards. He clawed through the dirt until he was embracing his backpack and the solid lump inside that was the codices' crystal.

"Cover! Take cover!" Li-Olsen threw himself behind a pillar as more flashes from the pulson stun weapons erupted. His two companions did the same, drawing weapons Callan recognized as solid-state particle cutters.

He spotted his rebreather abandoned on the ground nearby. It took him three tries to get it reattached to his face. Cool, clean air, blessedly free of grit, filled his lungs again.

"Sir! Get back!" El Tayib slithered up out of the crevasse, Yashida clinging to her. They'd clustered two climbing lines together and collaborated, each using a hand to ascend while El Tayib shot the Stratnorguards off of Callan with her heavy pulson.

Callan kept crawling. A keening whine cut the air. SSP cutter beams slashed overhead, their purple discharges glittering in the dusty clouds. The answering flash from the pulson El Tayib wielded was practically silent by comparison.

Yashida cried out. Callan peered through the blowing grit that abraded his skin. El Tayib and Yashida were slumped against each other at the gap between the stonework. Dark burn marks steamed on his Yashida's jumpsuit.

"Librarian! He's hit!" El Tayib shouted.

Whether the Stratnorguards intercepted their comms or not, Callan couldn't tell, but it seemed likely when they flung themselves around the pillar they'd been using for cover and rushed the position of the *Provenance* crew. Callan swept his pulson at the advancing figures and fired a steady burst their way, the white flash forming a long, wide beam rather than the nebulous bursts discharged by El Tayib's weapon.

The Stratnorguards dove into the dirt. The beam caught the third one, who was much bulkier than Li-Olsen, across the legs. The man grunted and slammed face-first onto the pathway.

A reddish hue grew brighter over the rim of cliffs. Callan hurried to El Tayib and Yashida. The bio readouts for Yashida's jump-suit appeared as a pale outline in his vision, with angry red warnings smothering Yashida's right shoulder, chest, and arm.

"Cardiac arrhythmia," Callan said. "The glancing blow from the SSP beam must have set it off. We need to stabilize his heart."

"Already on it." El Tayib left her pulson teetering on the edge of the stonework. She slapped a thick red C-pad module onto Yashida's chest. The second it had adhered to his jacket, hair-thin fibers shot out, stabbing deep through the fabric. The suit expelled self-sealing foam around the punctures.

"Clear," El Tayib warned. She pressed her palm to the C-pad. It let out a rising whine.

Yashida twitched and let out a guttural moan. His eyes looked glassy behind his mask. Callan held his breath as the lights flashing on the C-pad went from wobbly and irregular to steady, and didn't let it out until the bio readouts told him the temporary cardiac stabilization had been successful. He tried to ignore the smoldering brown scorch mark on the angled wall behind them, and the scorch marks on Yashida's jacket. If the beam had hit the pilot with anything more than a glancing blow, he would have died.

"Don't move." A weight pressed down on his back.

They were in no position to defend themselves. Callan slowly craned his neck. Li-Olsen had his SSP blaster wedged between Callan's shoulder blades. The woman, whose nameplate read "Mbatha," aimed her weapon at El Tayib.

"Put down the pulson."

Callan complied. "We need to get back to our shuttlewing."

"Yes, *we* do," Li-Olsen said, the tension tightening the pronunciation of his syllables. "Our lander wrecked, unfortunately. Give me the codices or we'll leave you here."

"I can't do that. It's my sworn duty to protect them."

"They don't even belong to you," Li-Olsen snapped.

"They don't belong to you, either," El Tayib said, "But at least we're not trying to atomize them."

"Ka-Thos descendants might live out among those stars," Callan said, but even as he said it, he knew it was a stretch of the truth meant to confuse the Stratnor officer. Library Intelligence would never intentionally direct Allied Archives. [INCOMPLETE SENTENCE — text appears to be missing here] "Even if we can't find them, we can share their knowledge with the galaxy. That freedom isn't something anyone has the right to stop."

"We have the right to take whatever measures we deem necessary to maintain order among human worlds of the Oversight Republic. You'd have alien ideas infect our way of life—"

"Sir." That from Mbatha. "The storm is closing faster than projected."

She was right. Callan saw the red electromagnetic discharges rippling along the far end of the valley. He checked his card blade, but it was awash with static. "Our comms are down," he said. "And I'm betting yours are, too."

"Again," Li-Olsen said, "We're taking your ship to orbit."

"I-if the storm's at the shuttlewing," Yashida gasped, "Sh-she's disabled. EMP surges here … She's not hardened against them."

"Quit talking. You need your strength to fly." El Tayib's tone was firm but tinged with worry.

"Li-Olsen, we can't make it to our ship." Callan knew he had to take the chance. He turned around the rest of the way, so that Li-Olsen's SSP blaster was centimeters from his chest. He couldn't see the other man's face behind the reflective visor, but he hoped he was as worried as he felt. "Get your man who's still out in the open over here. If he stays outside when the storm hits, the electromagnetic surge will fry his neurons as easily as our electronics."

"You're bluffing." Li-Olsen's voice shook with anger or fear, or perhaps both. "This won't become our tomb."

"It's not a tomb. It's a lifeboat." Callan pressed his hand against the nearest slanted stone and activated the embedded slicer. A broad, plate-like flake flopped off. He held it up so that Li-Olsen and the others could see the glittering crystal embedded across its surface, faint like a nebula's fringes. "This is the same crystalline structure as the object in which we found the codices stored. It's native to the planet and has properties that resist the electromagnetic flux. This is how the Ka-Thos were able to not only preserve the codices, but the writings inked on the walls inside."

Li-Olsen's aim was unwavering. A hiss grew over the roar of the storm. There was a strange pressure to the air around them, as if

Callan could feel the charged particles pressing against his clothing and his skin. His hair bristled.

"It's our only chance at survival," Callan said. "If you want to save your people."

Li-Olsen tilted his head. "Mbatha, get Sakuro. Bring him in here."

"But sir, if the *Trident* can't retrieve us—"

"I can't reach the *Trident*. Besides, if the enemy ship is still in orbit, the captain will have his hands full without worrying about us."

Callan suppressed a bleak laugh at the fact his enemies were in the same predicament, and were apparently governed by the same rules.

"Get him inside, now." Li-Olsen pressed a roundel inset on his mask. "Bot Three, determine the status of the enemy landing craft."

The sentrybot had stood there throughout the engagement, as motionless as one of the lopsided pillars. It turned and set off along the disappearing path, toward the rise over which the shuttlewing waited. Mbatha took Sakuro's arm and dragged him toward the gap in the stones. Sakuro clung to him, muttered imprecations filtering out of his mask. She came face to face with El Tayib.

"Help me lower my guy," El Tayib demanded, "then we'll get yours, because yours isn't suffering heart failure." She reached for the climbing line and began looping it around Yashida's midsection. Yashida barely stirred, his words reduced to incomprehensible murmurs by his wooziness as the C-pad pulsed his heart to keep it from malfunctioning any more than it had been.

Mbatha helped El Tayib, her motions stiff but just as urgent. El Tayib then slid down the slope, landing with a gentle thump below, and Mbatha eased Yashida along after her.

A distant sizzle of electronics made Callan look up. The sentrybot was a tiny figure wobbling at the top of the rise, on its way toward the shuttlewing. Sparks sputtered from its joints, and it stopped in its tracks, as dead and disabled as the other sentrybots El Tayib had shot with her pulson.

"Be grateful I used the wide beam low stun setting," Callan told Sakuro as he readjusted the bag containing the codices. "Or you'd be taking a nap throughout the entire presentation."

"*Blanknaz,*" Sakuro muttered. The man's legs were still incapacitated, but Li-Olsen assisted him as he pulled himself into a sitting position, while Mbatha turned her attention to him with a climbing line in hand.

Callan didn't know what the Stratnor insult meant but he opted to bear it proudly.

A curtain of red light washed over the valley. Churning electromagnetic discharges slashed from pillar to pillar, creating an overlapping web of impenetrable, intense lightning. The discharges buffeted Callan even a few hundred meters out. "Get down there," he told Li-Olsen. "Hurry."

The Stratnorguards did as instructed, with Li-Olsen and Mbatha guiding Sakuro down the slope. A warning echoed up from the depths, indecipherable to Callan but whatever was said, it slowed the Stratnorguards down. Callan waited until the tops of their heads were illuminated by the searchlight on El Tayib's pulson—no easy task with the winds whipping around him and the electrical discharges crinkling his jumpsuit—then pushed off.

He landed lightly in a crouch. The pressure from the storm eased even as the flashes reflected off the sides of the stones overhead. The entire buried structure trembled as the storm rolled over them. Callan held his breath. He hoped that everything he'd gleaned from the *Provenance*'s scans and the ancient records pieced together by Library Intelligence were right in their assessment of the Ka-Thos uses of this particular crystal—and its effectiveness.

He huddled next to El Tayib and placed a hand on her shoulder. She nodded, her pulson resting on her lap, as she clutched Yashida's hand in hers. The Stratnorguards clustered together on the other side of the cramped chamber, as far as they could get from Callan's team and the hissing, snarling storm above. Every so often an errant discharge would spark overhead, not making it deep into the crevasse they'd slid down but close enough Callan felt his heart skip.

"They haven't tried anything funny," El Tayib murmured. "I kept my pulson aimed at them as they came down. I think they thought I might stun them senseless and let them drop like rocks the rest of the way— especially if they pointed their weapons at me."

"What gave them that idea?" Callan grinned behind his mask.

"Because I told them." El Tayib made the end of the stun weapon waver as she pointed it at the Stratnor team again.

Callan checked the card blade and grimaced. Three minutes since the storm front had hit them. Ninety-two until it was past. He put the blade by his side and removed the codices from his bag, letting his beamlight play over its surface.

"What does it say?"

Li-Olsen's question startled Callan. He looked across at the Stratnorguard leader and found himself face to face with… well, a face. The reflective visor had split into three parts and folded back, revealing a rounded visage of mixed Caucasian and Asian heritage.

Hazel eyes watching Callan intently.

"I don't know," Callan said, "But eventually, I hope everyone will."

"And this is what you're risking your life for." Li-Olsen gestured at Yashida, whom El Tayib cradled. The pilot's face was pale, his eyes rimmed with red, but at least he was alert and talking. "What you risk your people's lives for. These … words."

"These words belonged to an entire world, one that went to a lot of trouble to save them when they knew everything else they valued was going to collapse." Callan touched the crystal gently. "We honor that by sharing what they knew with the rest of the galaxy. The same knowledge you want to destroy."

"Because it's dangerous," Li-Olsen insisted. "That's what we know. That's what we're trained to believe."

"Then maybe you'll find out just how true your belief is," Callan said.

Three hours later, well beyond the storm's estimated departure, pale pink light spilled into the opening. Callan was first up the climbing line, carrying the codices, with Li-Olsen right behind him.

The winds had abated. A gentle breeze, like the planet was whispering to Callan, ruffled his hair. The horizon was shot through with gold and orange, while the broad curve of the sky was a soft, pale rose.

Callan's blade pulsed with alerts. The first had to do with atmospheric conditions: the electrical disturbances had settled, and the air was within breathable tolerances. The second announced that a retrieval team was on its way.

He smiled at Li-Olsen. "I'm afraid our ride is here first."

Li-Olsen nodded. His eyebrows lifted and his frown deepened. He looked to Callan like a man who knew he'd lost the battle and, hopefully, had realized how foolish of a battle it was. Li-Olsen gestured at a blinking light on his wrist's gauntlet, onto which a comms device was embedded. "Yes, the *Trident* confirmed it has … Withdrawn to the outskirts of the Alguin star system."

Callan didn't ask what tonnage of Stratnor vessel the *Trident* was, but if a *Classifier* bookship scared it off, it had to be a patrol frigate or something smaller—and more lightly armed.

A familiar engine sound broke their oddly peaceful reverie. A pair of shuttlewings swept in from the west, one of which settled beyond the cliffs toward where Callan's ride had landed. The second one executed a sharp turn and a smooth drop to the top of the nearest cliff, its arrowhead shape shining in the late day's sun.

Smoke still drifted lazily from where the Stratnor lander had gone down. The sight brought up an uncomfortable question, but Callan asked it of Li-Olsen anyway. "Did you lose anyone?"

He watched as Li-Olsen's lips pressed into an even thinner line. A muscle tightened along his jaw. "Yes. Fernandez. Our pilot."

Callan thought of Yashida dozing under the influence of meds that El-Tayib had administered. The C-pad's indicators showed his heart rhythm was steady enough for transport. Permanent treatment aboard the *Provenance* would heal the damaged tissues. "I'm sorry. I am."

Li-Olsen nodded but said nothing.

Four people disembarked from the shuttlewing. Callan expected the trio of enlisted shelftechs with heavy pulsons like El Tayib carried but blinked from the surprise of watching Captain Belmont striding toward him. "Oh, boy," he muttered.

"Is that your deck officer?" Li-Olsen frowned, but after another second his eyes widened. "Wait, no. Those rank insignia—"

"She's the captain." Callan stood up as straight as he could, wishing he was a few centimeters taller.

"Good luck," Li-Olsen murmured as Belmont stopped in front of them.

She planted her hands on her hips. "What did I tell you when you left my bridge, Library Officer Sark?"

"Not to blow anything up and to keep my team alive, Ma'am."

Belmont shook her head. "And yet I hear you have wounded, a fried shuttlewing, and prisoners. In that order?"

"More or less, Captain." Callan avoided Li-Olsen's eyes. He didn't want to turn the man over, as ridiculous as it sounded, as if the Stratnor officer hadn't gotten Yashida wounded, and tried to kill the rest of them.

"More or less." Belmont shook her head.

"But, ma'am—"

She held up a single finger. Callan waited a few seconds. "But what?" she finally asked.

"Technically, Captain, I didn't blow anything up."

Li-Olsen snorted.

"Well then, it seems this isn't a complete disaster." Belmont finally seemed to notice him. She looked him up and down, disdain creasing her face,then gestured to the shelftechs forming a cordon around them. "Take this man into custody. He's to remain an FWI prisoner until we can arrange to deliver him to his people under a flag of truce."

"Captain, there's two more of his people down below with Yashida and El Tayib," Callan said.

"You heard the man," Belmont said to he

landing party. "Bring everyone up and bind the two Stratnorguards."

"Yes, ma'am."

One of the enlisted crew approached Li-Olsen, who offered his wrists pressed together. A pair of magnetic binding strips interlocked around his arms.

"Captain, wait." Callan stepped to Li-Olsen's side and dug in his pocket for the book. He pulled it free with a swish of card stock against fabric. "Here, Lieutenant. For you."

"To … what?" Li-Olsen scowled as the rest of the *Provenance* landing party headed for the makeshift shelter of the ruined Codex Septon. "Read? That's not my job."

"Stratnor won't agree to any prisoner exchange for a while. Probably a few weeks." Belmont smiled at Callan. "It's your call. Just make sure he returns it on time from our brig."

She strode off to investigate the situation in the ruins. Callan flipped through the book's pages and found the section he wanted:

"How many it had cost in the amassing, what blood and sorrow, what good ships scuttled on the deep, what brave men walking the plank, what shot of cannon, what shame and lies and cruelty, perhaps no man alive could tell."

Li-Olsen's scowl remained, but he took the book in his bound hands. "*Treasure Island.* That doesn't seem like a secure holding facility."

"Read it. I promise, it's worth it," Callan said over his shoulder as he followed Captain Belmont. "I'll let you know when it's due."

Nineteen days later, Callan stood at the observation viewport of Drai Ghell-Adams Starport, drumming his fingers on the red metal railing. The *Provenance* sat framed in the oblong window, its pearly white hull gleaming under the lights of the station.

"You look pale," Akello said from beside him.

He chuckled, then wiped his palms on his

trousers. Pale? Callan was surprised he hadn't thrown up. "This is the most nerve-wracking part of any retrieval, I think."

"Not skipping through space at hundreds of times the speed of light?" Akello smiled slyly. "Or engaging a shootout with Stratnor burn squads? Or nearly crashing in a storm?"

Callan shrugged. "Okay, you make good points, ma'am." But he still couldn't tear his gaze away from the bookship as the upper curve of the hull recessed, then slid open. Giant magnetic clamps lowered from the rail overhead, slowly, meter by meter, toward the bookship. Meanwhile, a shining black and gold structure rose from inside the *Provenance,* its rounded edges peeking over the top of the hull.

The library was coming home.

Callan held his breath as the magnetic clamps locked into place atop the module. Green lights pulsed. It was secure.

"I understand Mr. Yashida has made a full recovery," Akello said.

"He did. I'm glad ..." Callan frowned as he searched for the words he needed. "This work shouldn't cost lives. One man died. That's too many, and it shouldn't matter what side he's on. There shouldn't be a side."

"I understand, but the galaxy is not, unfortunately, as black and white a place as we would all like it to be."

"But we've been trying for so long to change it."

"And we may have to try a while longer." Akello pointed at the library module as the clamps pulled it nearer to the starport. "In the meantime, we safeguard what knowledge we can. But from what I understand of your narrative entry, you have taken steps beyond what most are willing."

Footsteps approached them from behind. Commander Aguilar strode over to the rail. "The library module docking should be complete in about twenty minutes. We'll run a check on the atmospheric seals and the power conduit connections, but my guess is you'll be able to open up shop by 1445 hours."

"We have announced through the starport network an opening time of 1500 hours, Commander, so that is gratifying to hear."

Akello touched Callan's arm. "The Second Librarian and I will be there to greet our patrons."

"Good deal." Aguilar smiled. "And Mr. Sark? Your pal has requested one visit."

"My pal?" Callan blinked at him. If Yashida was back on his feet, nothing would stop him from touring the library like anyone else.

"Stratnor Lieutenant Li-Olsen. He even begged to put off the prisoner transfer by twenty-four hours." Aguilar shrugged, the overhead lights making his scar tissue seem to move. "Never saw anything like it before, Mr. Sark, so you must have done all right. Worth the risk?"

Callan looked past him at the library module as it disappeared from view. A few seconds later, a distant impact made the deck beneath him tremble. He didn't know what Li-Olsen's request meant, but it was something out of the ordinary, something beyond the fight.

"Yes, sir," Callan said, "I'd say it was."

By that evening, word had spread throughout the starport. Hundreds of people from nine species gathered at the curved wall of the library module, which trundled slowly open, revealing the treasure trove of the entire ship's archives.

The Codex Septon of the Ka-Thos was the centerpiece past which everyone walked.

Callan's hands flew across his console as he registered videos and gave out access codes, but his gaze kept jumping to the codices, now free of their protective crystal. A tall column of clear plastic, filled with a preservative atmosphere, kept them from further degrading. Printed copies of translated versions flew from the shelves as everyone checked out what was available—humans from all corners of known space; the four-armed, long-faced Ghiqasu who made up the bulk of the Pan-Stellar Consociation's population and dominated security forces; a smattering of diminutive, tentacled Rycole.

Akello and other library crew conversed with the visitors. Shelftechs led them deeper into the stacks, where they could access more translated works the *Provenance* had discovered and reproduced during months in deep space.

Callan was watching for one person in particular, though, and had just about given up four hours later when a pair of *Provenance* security guards in thick body armor escorted Li-Olsen to his desk.

The Stratnor officer looked worn down, despite the fairly comfortable secured cabin he'd occupied. He'd been kept more as a guest than a prisoner.

"Lieutenant." Callan nodded. "It's good to see you again. I understand your people won't be here to get you for a little while longer. What's your plan until then?"

Li-Olsen wore a single-piece jumpsuit, with only two pockets. The bright yellow garment was designed to keep him from harming himself or anyone else; he'd get his uniform back when the prisoner transfer took place. He dug into one pocket, the motion rendered awkward by the magnetic binders clamping his wrists together.

His hands emerged clasping *Treasure Is-*

land.

"I finished it," Li-Olsen said. He held it out to Callan. "And I'm going to need to see what else is in there."